DAVIE'S WEE DOG
&
RORY THE ROEBUCK

Davie's Wee Dog

WILLIAM MACKELLAR

Illustrated by Barry Wilkinson

&

Rory the Roebuck

DAVID STEPHEN

Illustrated by Don Higgins

NEW ACORN LIBRARY

THE BODLEY HEAD

LONDON · SYDNEY · TORONTO

© William MacKellar 1957 and
© David Stephen 1961
Illustrations © The Bodley Head Ltd
1965 and 1961
ISBN 0 370 10998 8
Printed in Great Britain for
The Bodley Head Ltd
9 Bow Street, London WC2E 7AL
by BAS Printers Ltd, Wallop, Hampshire
Filmset in Monophoto Plantin
This edition first published 1975

Davie's Wee Dog was first published by the McGraw-Hill
Book Company, Inc., as *Wee Joseph*, in 1957, and was
first published in Great Britain in the Bodley Head
Acorn Library in 1965. *Rory the Roebuck* was first
published in the Bodley Head Acorn Library in 1961.

CONTENTS

Davie's Wee Dog

WILLIAM MACKELLAR

Illustrated by Barry Wilkinson

For my father
John MacKellar

I

Davie Buys a Dog

Davie's eyes popped in his head. A slow pounding came from under his blue wool jersey where his heart was. Again he looked into Mr Blaikie's face. And again he looked at the squirming little creature that the farmer held in his hands.

'And you want only sixpence for him?' he repeated.

'That's all, Davie Campbell,' the farmer said heartily. 'And a fine beast he is too.'

Davie felt his breath strangle in his throat. He put out his hands. The farmer placed the little dog between the cupped fingers. For a long moment Davie just stood, too filled with emotion to speak. Gently he eased his forefinger down the little dog's back. It was strange how thin and uneven the fur was. Still he was only a pup. That would explain it.

'Aye, it's the fine one he is,' Mr Blaikie said. 'The fine one indeed.' He winked slyly at the boy. 'I've been saving him for yourself, Davie Campbell.'

The boy nodded but did not answer. He had

never liked Mr Blaikie very much. As a matter of fact he couldn't recall anyone in the whole village of Stranmore ever having said anything kind about the farmer. Still it was good of him to have saved the little pup just for him. Just went to show how wrong people could be about other people sometimes.

Again Davie's finger trailed across the pup's skimpy coat. It was queer how many colours it had. Most dogs that Davie had seen had only two colours. *This* little pup—why, it was a rainbow of all kinds of hues—white and black and brown and russet and pink! Surely there had never been such a wonderfully coloured dog!

'Aye, it's the grand dog he is for certain, Mr Blaikie,' he agreed. 'Will you look at the rare markings on him? I'm thinking there will not be many like him in these parts.'

Mr Blaikie laughed as though Davie had just said something very funny. 'Aye, he's different, I'll say *that* for him. A rare kind as you rightly said, Davie Campbell.'

'And you want only sixpence for him, Mr Blaikie?'

The farmer nodded. His eyes, too close together,

narrowed slightly. His face no longer wore its smile of good humour when he spoke.

'You've got the money?' he snapped. 'But of course you have! Or why would you be asking for the wee dog?' He stretched out his big hand and waited.

Davie hesitated. The sixpence in his pocket was a lot of money. It was everything he had—the sum of all his work for the past month. His father would be angry at first when he learned it had been spent. But when he caught sight of the wee dog, he would understand. Holding the pup in one hand, Davie dug his fingers into the pocket of his trousers. Slowly he withdrew the small silver coin and dropped it into the farmer's hand. Mr Blaikie's crafty face was all smiles again.

'Mind you take good care of him!' He chuckled as he turned away. 'There will not be many like him in these parts.'

Suddenly he laughed again, just as he had laughed before. Davie could see nothing funny in what he had said. Still, if Mr Blaikie wanted to laugh that was *his* business. Anyway who cared? For a moment he watched as the farmer turned and walked away. Then his eyes went to the small bundle of uneven fur that lay cradled in his hands. A great joy rose like a hot flame in Davie Campbell. Tenderly he poked his finger under a round, pink nose. He was rewarded a moment later when a small red tongue curled out and took a solemn lick at his finger.

'Aye,' he said huskily. 'It's plain to see you're a grand dog. A grand dog, indeed!'

Again Davie ran his fingers admiringly over the pup's body. It was strange, though, how close the ribs seemed to be against the coat; almost as if there were no flesh at all on the wee body, as if the pup had been starved. But who would ever starve a fine dog like this now? Davie dismissed the thought at once.

'I'll call you Joseph,' he said suddenly, and knew that of all names, *this* was the right one. For hadn't they just read last week in Sunday school about Joseph and his coat of many colours?

'Joseph,' he said softly. 'I'm talking to you, Joseph.'

The freckled nose wrinkled. A gangling ear twitched ever so slightly. A moist brown eye winked open.

'He knows his name already,' marvelled Davie.

Pride made the words tight in his throat.

2

Mr Leckie Disapproves

The scent of the bog myrtle rode the soft hill wind and moved with a slow sweetness in Davie's nostrils. Joseph lay crooked in his arms as he started the journey back to his home. Davie's bare feet moved easily through the coarse, dry heather. When first he had doffed his shoes with the coming of the warm June days, the bracken fronds and the spiky heather shoots had seemed harsh against his feet. Now he could take even the thorniest under-growth in stride. He hummed as he walked.

'Good day to you, Davie,' a man called from a small granite house with trim green shutters.

'Good day to you, Mr Leckie,' Davie said to the schoolmaster.

The teacher leaned on the gate leading to his garden and smiled.

'What do you have there, Davie?'

Davie smiled back proudly. 'A dog, Mr Leckie. And it's a fine dog he is too!'

'H-m.' Mr Leckie's lips pursed slightly as he

looked at the dog. 'Where did you get him, Davie?'

'From Mr Blaikie.' He stopped. He knew there was something else he should say. 'For sixpence.'

'For sixpence?' A shadow fell across the schoolteacher's face. 'May I look at him, Davie?'

Carefully the boy handed the dog over. 'His name's Joseph.'

'H-m.' Again Mr Leckie's lips set in a tight line. His long fingers moved slowly over the dog. The shadow darkened on his face.

'You paid sixpence for him, you said?'

'Aye.'

'I see.' With a little grunt the schoolmaster returned the dog to the boy. 'I'm afraid our Mr Blaikie is as big a rascal as people say he is.'

Davie stopped, his hands around Joseph. 'What do you mean?'

'Just that this Joseph of yours isn't quite the fine dog Mr Blaikie claimed he was.'

Davie stared, then leaped to defend Joseph. 'Are you saying he's not got the grand blood at all?'

The schoolmaster let his hand drop gently on Davie's shoulder. 'I'm afraid he's just a mongrel, Davie. This dog was evidently one of a large litter. The mother couldn't take care of him. Mr Blaikie didn't bother. Why just look at the poor thing, Davie! He's skin and bones!'

'But he's only a wee pup,' Davie protested. 'Besides, why should Mr Blaikie see that the other pups were fed and not Joseph?'

Mr Leckie sighed. 'Tastes in dogs differ, Davie. Your taste is the right one for you. However, most people wouldn't like Joseph. All his markings are in the wrong places. And he's got the oddest colours I've ever seen. Besides, his legs are too short and his body is too long and his ears don't match. Why, you'd think they had been meant for two different dogs.' He shook his head sadly. 'I'm afraid, Davie,' he said, 'most people would call Joseph a misfit.'

'A mis . . .?' Davie clamped his jaws tight to contain the bitter word. Not Joseph! His blue eyes blazed fiercely as he backed away from the schoolteacher and held Joseph in his arms.

'As you said before, Mr Leckie, it's a matter of taste. Good day to you.' Quickly he turned away.

Mr Leckie called after him. 'Good day to you too, Davie.'

What was the matter with the man, thought Davie angrily. Aye, and him a schoolteacher too!

Calling Joseph a misfit! It was a wonder Joseph hadn't leaped at his throat. Aye, a wonder indeed! He lifted his arms and held his face close to Joseph. He could feel the soft warmth steal up from the pup's body. The coarse hair moved ever so gently against Davie's cheek in time with the scrawny little creature's breathing.

Joseph was fast asleep.

3

Enter Tam Menzies

Davie had stopped to rest by a mossy dike, smothered in a net of white hawthorns, when Joseph stirred and woke. Gently the boy placed the pup down on the ground. He watched with delight from his rocky perch as Joseph moved through the long grass.

Actually he didn't move *through* the grass as much as he moved *over* it. It may have been because of his short legs or his lack of strength to bend back the tough reeds. Or perhaps it was just that Joseph wanted to see where he was going. *That* was it, thought Davie. He sat on the dike, his bare feet dangling, and followed Joseph's freckled nose rising and falling through the thick grass and heather. Finally, Joseph trotted back to where Davie sat.

After halting by a small spring and swallowing the tooth-numbing cold water, they continued on their way. The ground was rough and thick with briars and bramble bushes. Davie took the pup in his arms. They had still a number of miles to go before they reached home. He sang as he walked, for he had forgotten all about Mr Leckie.

> *Will ye no come back again,*
> *Will ye no, Prince Charlie?*
> *Better loved ye canna be,*
> *Will ye no come back again?*

Why he should sing of Bonnie Prince Charlie was hard to say. It was just that, with Joseph in his arms, it *seemed* only right to sing. And when your heart puts a song on your lips you don't argue. You just sing. So Davie sang.

> *Better loved ye canna be,*
> *Will ye no come back again?*

Of course it was true that after the battle on Culloden Moor Bonnie Prince Charlie had hidden in this very glen. Every schoolboy in the village knew the story—how the Prince had fled in the night with the Duke of Cumberland's soldiers at his heels and had lain hidden all night in the cold mists of Ben Ulva, the huge mountain at the head of the glen. With the morning light the Prince had escaped to the Hebrides.

Ben Ulva still sat at the head of the glen, looking like a huge whale trapped in a fine net of silvery mist. Yet it was no longer the same mountain that the last of the Stuarts had looked at. Progress had come to the Highlands. A thin line of metal pylons marched in single file up the mountain. Davie could see the workmen, in the distance like tiny ants busy at their tasks. He knew what these tasks were. The Government had decided to open up the Highlands—to tame the wild rivers and the floods, to bring cheap power and electricity. Life would be easier for all.

Davie had just swung over the crest of the small hill when he heard the shrill skirl. So suddenly did it come that for a moment he felt the blood turn cold in his veins. Then he smiled. Of course! Old Tam Menzies, the hermit. Tam lived on the farm over the hill. Everyone thought he was crazy, but

Davie knew better. Tam just thought things out differently.

The high thin skirl of the bagpipes drew nearer. Then from behind a screen of pine trees stepped an old man. His hair was a long white train in the wind. His cheeks as he puffed were two bright red apples. He paused when he saw Davie, and the air in the chanter and drones of the pipes choked and became still.

'A good day to you, Davie Campbell,' he said in a high-pitched voice.

'A good day to you, Mr Menzies,' Davie returned civilly.

The hermit stood on tiptoe and craned his neck forward.

'What have you got there, Davie lad?' he cried shrilly. 'There's something hidden in that hand of yours. I'll bet a shilling on it.' His little eyes seemed to climb over Davie's hand.

'A dog.'

'A dog, no less?'

'Aye.'

The old hermit's face wrinkled with pleasure. Tenderly he took the pup from Davie. He parted the floppy ears and tickled Joseph's head.

'My!' he breathed, his eyes aglow. 'Is he not the grand wee dog?'

'He is that!' Davie acknowledged proudly. He smiled with his eyes at the hermit. What a knowing old man he was! And yet they called him crazy!

'A fine dog he is, eh, Davie? Aye, but that's for certain. It's plain to see there's the grand blood in him.'

Davie's red head bobbed in quick agreement. 'Aye, for certain.' How clever of the old man to have spotted Joseph's worth so quickly! Suddenly he remembered Mr Leckie, remembered the cruel things that he had said. The boy looked open-faced at his friend. If anybody knew, it would be Tam Menzies.

'And how can you tell for certain, Mr Menzies?' he asked anxiously.

'Eh? Tell what, lad?'

'That there's the grand blood in him?'

'Oh, that now.' The hermit scratched his long nose thoughtfully. He whistled between his thin lips. He frowned. He turned Joseph carefully over and squinted through one eye at him. Then he laughed merrily. He dug a bony finger playfully into Davie's ribs.

'How can you tell what's a rowan tree and what's not a rowan tree? Answer me that, Davie Campbell.'

The boy frowned. He had seen hundreds of rowan trees. He recognized them as soon as he saw them. But how did he know for certain? Somehow the old man's question wasn't so easy to answer as it seemed.

'I'm not sure at all, Mr Menzies,' he said truthfully. 'It's just that somehow a rowan tree *looks* like what a rowan tree should be.'

'Right!' squealed old Tam triumphantly. 'And that's the same with the wee dog here! He looks like a dog would look that had the grand blood in him. And what better proof will you be wanting, lad, than that?' The hermit's pale blue eyes seemed to be doing a Highland fling of delight in his head. Old Tam prided himself on his logic.

Davie took back Joseph and set him on the ground. How right he had been about old Tam Menzies! Crazy? Why, there was no one sharper in all Scotland!

When they had gone a few hundred yards along, Davie turned and looked back and waved. Old Tam Menzies was standing on a rock. The wind made a halo of his white hair. He raised a thin bony arm in farewell. Then he lifted the blowpipe to his lips. The high skirl of the pipes carried faintly to Davie's ears across the glen.

The boy turned again and waved back gratefully to his friend. Old Tam Menzies crazy? Why, he didn't even *look* crazy.

4

Waiting in the Cottage

Nell Campbell looked at her son. There was surprise in her eyes. There was pain there too, but Davie didn't see it.

'A dog, Davie?' she said. She stared at the little creature with the queer blotches of colour.

'Aye. I got him from Mr Blaikie for sixpence.'

'For sixpence?'

He looked up quickly, sensing the distress in her voice. 'He's worth it—aye, and more,' he said stoutly. He watched as Joseph greedily sank his tongue into the saucer of milk. The puppy made queer little slurpings of pleasure as his tongue scooped up the milk.

'His name's Joseph,' Davie said when his mother didn't speak.

'Joseph?'

'Aye, like him in the Bible. The one with the coat with all the colours.'

She smiled just a little sadly. Her fingers were a familiar softness on Davie's red hair, like no other softness in all the world.

'Davie, Davie,' she murmured, her face very close to his. 'In many ways he was not a very happy man, that Joseph of yours. I'm thinking your wee dog is too well named.'

He felt her fingers tighten on his shoulder. He looked up and could feel the sudden coldness that cramped his stomach.

'And why?' he said. Although now he knew with a terrible sureness what the answer would be.

'Your father, Davie.' She rushed on lest he should misunderstand. 'It's a just man he is, and kind in many ways, Davie. In ways you're too young to know. But he fights hard to put the bread in our mouths. And he can't abide the vanities of the world.'

'Vanities!' cried Davie, pointing his finger at Joseph. 'You call Joseph a vanity?'

She let the little smile have its way with her mouth. 'Joseph is a fine wee dog. But we'll not be able to use him. And if we'll not be able to use him, I'm afraid'—her voice sank to a whisper—'we'll not be able to keep him.' She paused. 'I'm sorry, Davie.'

He did not answer. What answer was there to give? Or what meaning could there be in any answer? It was his father who would say what should be. Or what should not be. His father, that tall dark man with the stern eyes and the sterner mouth. The sombre man who worked from early dawn to sunset to scrape a living from the flinty soil. Ian Campbell was not a man who smiled often. Or often had much to smile about.

Davie sat in the kitchen with Joseph and waited. He had given the dog a few scraps of meat and made a little bed of rags and straw for him. Into this Joseph had climbed and, curling up in a ball, had fallen fast asleep.

The hours passed slowly. Davie's mother worked quietly in the light by the window, her needle moving swiftly, endlessly. With the late afternoon sun glinting on the mirror over the big dresser, she rose to get the supper ready. The heavy smell of the bubbling pot of broth steamed the room. A griddle of scones hung over the ruddy peat fire.

She did not speak to Davie. Davie did not speak to her. Other than her movements the only sound in the kitchen was the *ticktock, ticktock* of the old wall clock.

The shadows lengthened in the room. The flames became brighter in the hearth. The tiny dust whorls no longer slid down the slanting rays of sunlight. The gloom seemed a living thing—a great evil fog creeping into every nook and cranny—until finally there was no hiding place. Not even in a small boy's heart.

The oil lamp on the table had just been lit when Davie's brothers, Murdoch and Jimmy, came in. Murdoch and Jimmy were men. Murdoch, long-jawed and dark, was eighteen. Jimmy, square-faced and fair, was sixteen. They stared in amazement when they spotted the dog.

'Am I dreaming!' Murdoch exclaimed. He pointed a big finger. 'What's that?'

Davie was on his feet between Murdoch and the dog. '*That* is Joseph,' he said defiantly. 'And he's mine.'

There was a sudden silence. A fire-charred peat fell with a slushing sound into the ashes at the bottom of the grate. 'Yours?' Murdoch asked.

'Aye.'

'And does your father know this?' It was Jimmy who asked the question.

Ever so slightly Davie moved his head. 'No.'

'Ah!' The older brothers seemed to say it together. Their eyes met and Jimmy laughed a little nervously and patted Davie roughly on the head.

'Good luck to you, Davie,' he said simply.

Murdoch grunted but said nothing. Yet from time to time his eyes travelled slowly to Joseph and then to Davie. Once he shook his head.

The light from the oil lamp flickered in the kitchen. Little puddles of brightness splashed up and down the pine-panelled wall. Jimmy whistled off key as he washed. Jimmy never whistled before eating. His whistling sounded strange in Davie's ears.

Suddenly Jimmy's pursed lips froze. The air between his teeth was still. He cocked his head towards the door. But Davie had already heard. Heard the heavy sound of the foot on the gravel outside the door. He felt his heartbeat grow big in his chest. His father had come home!

The door opened and the cold night air rushed

in. Then Ian Campbell entered. He stood there for a long moment, his big shoulders bowed, his deep-set eyes bleak with weariness. Then he looked up and saw Joseph. He stopped where he was.

'What is this?' he said. He closed the door behind him.

5

Ian Campbell Meets Joseph

'Now, Ian,' Nell Campbell said with a show of brightness, 'there's no reason at all to look so surprised. It's just a wee dog that Davie brought home.'

'We have no room for dogs here,' Ian Campbell said. 'Nor food either, I'm thinking.' He shrugged off his work jacket and tossed it over a straight-backed chair. He frowned at Joseph, asleep in his box.

'Where did you get this beast, Davie?' he asked calmly.

He did not look angry. Encouraged, Davie told the story of how he had got Joseph from Mr Blaikie. At first he had meant to hide the fact that he had paid for him. Now, with Joseph's worth at stake, he thought it best to mention the sixpence that the dog cost him.

'Aye, but he's worth it, he is,' the boy finished. 'For he's a fine dog!' He stopped, knowing there should be something else he should say. 'Aye, and it's the great help he'll be around the house.'

The silence was thick in the kitchen. It seemed to drip from the very beams in the ceiling. Then it was torn asunder by the sound of his father's voice.

'You paid sixpence for the like of that! Hard-earned money thrown away sinfully to a rogue and a thief like Blaikie! Could you not have seen that the dog is worthless?'

The voice was a terrible loudness in Davie's ears. It was hard to think. There was a queer spinning and tumbling in his mind, and it was impossible to sort the words out. The words that needed to be spoken if Joseph were to stay.

'Have you no tongue?' Ian Campbell said.

'He's not worthless! I don't care what you think!' And now that the words were there, the courage was there too. He looked with defiance at this man whom he feared and was beginning to hate. 'There's the grand blood in him. Mr Blaikie said so. Aye, and so did old Tam Menzies!'

Little points of light stabbed at the darkness in Ian Campbell's eyes. For a moment his big hand went up and Davie felt a quick weakness in his legs as he waited for the blow to fall. But no blow fell. Davie blinked his eyes open.

'It is well for you, Davie, that I am slow to anger,' Ian Campbell said between thin lips. He breathed deeply, and his outgoing breath was a soft rasp in the heavy air. 'I am not in the habit of reasoning with my sons. Yet I would not want you to think I am unjust.' He stopped and closed his eyes with a quick tiredness. 'I am a very just man, Davie.'

'Then be just with Joseph here!' Davie pleaded.

Ian Campbell nodded. His dark face was calm again. The sudden tiredness gone. He pointed to a chair. 'Do you see that chair, Davie?'

He nodded. 'Aye.'

'And what will it be for?'

'To sit on.'

'And those shoes under the bed?'

'To put on your feet.'

'And that plate, Davie?'

'To eat from.'

Ian Campbell stopped. 'They all have a purpose, eh?'

'Aye.'

'They all have a use?'

'Aye.'

Ian Campbell's long finger stabbed forward and pointed straight at Joseph. 'And what of that miserable beast? What purpose—aye, what use is *he*?' His voice cracked like a lash, and Davie flinched.

'He—he—' the boy floundered. He tried hard to think of something to say on Joseph's behalf. Somehow Joseph didn't have any purpose, really. Except maybe to make the world a little brighter by just being in it.

'I'm waiting, Davie.'

He looked again at the dog. 'I just like him,' he said gravely. Somehow there didn't seem to be anything more one could add to that.

'Vain affection!' thundered Ian Campbell. His brow was black. 'This is no useful dog! It's but a cur for preening and sinful pampering! Our bread is hard earned, Davie Campbell. I will not have it used to feed a useless beast. Do you hear that?'

'Aye,' he said. His voice was a small dryness in his throat. He did not look at his father.

'Good,' Ian Campbell said grimly. He paused,

then said with a quick mildness, 'You can keep him here for the night. There will be no harm in it.'

Davie did not answer. There was nothing to say. Joseph still slept. What was it his mother had said? *'In many ways he was not a very happy man, that Joseph of yours. I'm thinking your wee dog was too well named.'*

His mother was right, of course. Joseph hadn't been the happiest of men. With his coat of many colours he had been sold into slavery. He had known hunger. He had known loneliness. He had been in prison. Yet in the end everything had worked out well.

Somehow the thought was a slight comfort to Davie as he took his place at the table.

6

Davie Gets His Orders

While Murdoch and Jimmy exchanged small talk at the table, Nell Campbell poured out the bowls of steaming broth. She sliced the bread that she had made the day before and gave Davie the half with the white crust that he loved so much. Usually he would dip it into the broth until it was soggy. Then, while it still dripped barley and leeks and peas he would let his teeth sink into the warm, sweet softness. But tonight Davie let the bread lie where it was.

When the tea was poured, Davie's mother put the scones and oatcakes on the table. Davie nibbled moodily at the oatcake. The nutty paste was coarse against his tongue as the cake crumbled and melted in his mouth. Around him he heard the voices of the others. They seemed remote and distant. Once Jimmy laughed. Then the dishes were gathered up and the family pulled itself into a tight semicircle around the blazing fireplace.

'You can give the dog a bit of the meat, Davie, if you've a mind to,' Ian Campbell said as he sank into the ancient leather armchair.

Davie, who had already hidden away several choice pieces, did not reply. He cut up the food into tiny pieces and placed them in a clean tin saucer. He watched as Joseph's little jaws busily set to work. The dog was hungry and licked the saucer clean in a matter of seconds. Davie gave him a little more meat, then, fearful that his father might think that Joseph ate like this *all* the time,

set a dish of water before him. Joseph drank noisily, his long ears just missing the water.

After a while Ian Campbell laid down the book he was reading. His mind seemed far away as he gazed fixedly at the dancing flames in the hearth.

'Tomorrow, Davie, you will take the beast back to Mr Blaikie. You will ask him for the sixpence. It's not in his nature to give it back, I'm thinking. Be that as it will, you will still return the wee dog to him. Is that clear?'

'Aye.' Davie's voice was low. He pulled his hand gently back and forth across Joseph's skimpy coat. The dog seemed to tremble and whimper and draw closer to Davie's hand. *He knows*, thought Davie. He was suddenly aware that his father was still speaking.

'—and if Mr Blaikie will not give you the sixpence and will not take the dog back, then you had better see that someone else gets him. For, mark my words, Davie, this dog has no place in this house. *No* place. Do you understand that?'

Davie's lips twitched just enough to let the word out. 'Aye.'

'Good.' Ian Campbell's eyes returned to the book in his hands.

While Jimmy chattered and laughed and Murdoch worked over a split bamboo salmon rod the evening slid quietly away. Nell Campbell's needle rose and fell, rose and fell. Joseph, after sniffing his way around the kitchen a few times, made his way back to where Davie lay on the floor. Ian Campbell read. The peats changed colour in the fireplace. The little tide of ashes lapped higher in the hearth.

Suddenly Ian Campbell closed his book. He pressed his big hands against the arms of the chair and eased himself to his feet. His bulk cut across the light from the fireplace. The shadow fell directly on where Joseph lay curled up on the floor.

Davie felt the quick coldness press against his heart, almost as though a door had suddenly opened and let in the night air. His father's rising from his chair meant only one thing. The day had come to an end.

Davie got to his feet. It was time for bed. The day was over. This was the day that had brought Joseph to him. Now it was finished. When he woke in the morning there would be a new day waiting— a day that would take Joseph away from him.

7

No Home for Joseph

Mr Blaikie laughed, a high shrill laugh without any humour in it.

'On your way, Davie Campbell!' he cried. 'The wee dog is yours, fairly sold and fairly bought.'

'It's not just the sixpence,' Davie said. 'My father said you can keep the sixpence. He—he says you should keep Joseph, too.'

'Keep him?' The farmer laughed again. When he laughed the suety flesh moved in his face and seemed to bury the small, darting eyes. 'What kind of a fool do you think I am, Davie Campbell? Waste honest food on a thing like *that*!' He pointed a scornful finger at Joseph.

Davie stared. 'But didn't you say yourself he was a fine dog?'

The farmer chuckled deep in his throat. He pushed Davie forward with a rough hand. 'Now get along with you! There's work to be done.'

Davie fell back a few steps. All at once he felt the quick fear that crept up his spine on cold rat feet. If Mr Blaikie wouldn't take the pup for *nothing* what would become of Joseph? Suppose *everybody* in Stranmore felt the same way? Davie watched as Mr Blaikie turned and went back to his farm. It just couldn't be! Somebody would surely want Joseph!

It was not until two full hours later, after having knocked at every door in Stranmore, that he finally realized that *nobody* wanted Joseph. It was not that most of the people weren't kind. They were. And it wasn't that some of them weren't looking for a dog. They were. It was just that when they saw Joseph they seemed to lose interest. A few had even laughed, and asked where on earth he had ever got such a dog. But in the end the result was always the same. Nobody wanted Joseph.

Davie walked away from the village with Joseph at his heels. He followed his feet blindly through the rough country. Hot tears scalded his eyes at the corners. Finally he reached a small hollow behind a row of scrawny pine trees. He flung himself forward and buried his face in the tall grass. Small sobs shook his shoulders.

After a while he stirred and drew an angry sleeve across his eyes. This was no time for crying. It was a time for thinking—for thinking what to do about Joseph. The little dog lay panting by his feet, his mouth open, his small pink tongue showing.

'There's got to be a way, Joseph, there's just got to!' he whispered.

He closed his eyes in an effort to think more clearly. It was strange how when one shut one's eyes, one's ears seemed to open. As he lay on his stomach he could hear the wind whisper through the blades of grass. The lazy hum of the bees drowsing among the clover carried to his ears. From far away came the peevish cry of a lapwing. And then suddenly there was another sound, high and shrill, and then a cackle of laughter.

'If it's not Davie Campbell, himself, and his bonnie wee dog.'

Davie blinked his eyes open. It was old Tam Menzies.

8

Of Faith and Mustard Seeds

The hermit listened, bright-eyed and solemn as Davie told his story. From time to time the old man tugged at his ear as though in deep thought. He scratched his head when Davie had finished.

'A hard problem you give me, Davie.'

'Aye, but are you not the clever one, Mr Menzies?' Davie pointed out. 'Are you forgetting that?'

'True, true,' the hermit said quickly. 'I have a rare cleverness. I'm glad you reminded me of it.' He frowned again and tugged nervously at his long, crooked nose. Suddenly his gentle eyes brightened.

'I've got it, laddie! I'll take the wee dog! Then you can come and see him whenever you've a mind to!' He wheezed with pleasure. 'How will *that* be for clever thinking, Davie Campbell?'

The boy was just about to let out a whoop of delight when he remembered something. He shook his head slightly.

'I'm afraid my father will not let you have Joseph,' he said. He didn't quite know how to go on without hurting his old friend. 'He—he'll not be knowing you as well as I do.'

Tam Menzies nodded. 'Aye, he'll be thinking I'm daft, is that it, Davie?'

'Aye.' He did not look at the hermit.

'But you don't think I'm daft, now, do you?'

The boy shook his head. 'I think you are the clever one for certain. In all Stranmore it was only you that saw the grand blood in Joseph.'

'Aye, that was clever of Tam Menzies, was it not?' the old man said, pleased.

'Anyway,' said Davie with a frown, 'we've got to think of something.'

'I just *thought* of something,' the old man pointed out, a slightly hurt look on his face. 'Now you want me to think again.'

'Sorry.'

'It's not easy to think clever twice in a row,' grumbled the hermit.

'Even once in a row is hard,' Davie said politely.

'Aye, it is that. Even for Tam Menzies. Now let me see, Davie, let me see.' His frown seemed to tug his whole face out of shape. Suddenly his long fingers cracked.

'I've done it again, Davie!' he croaked in

triumph. 'I've thought clever twice in a row!' He laughed shrilly and clapped his hands in glee.

'What is the clever thought this time?' Davie asked eagerly.

The old man grinned. 'Find the mustard seed.'

Davie stared. For one moment he almost was afraid his old friend *was* crazy.

'Find the what, Mr Menzies?'

'Mustard seed. Mustard seed,' the hermit said a little crossly. 'I read about it a long time ago in the Bible. It says if you have faith like a grain of mustard seed, you can do anything. Aye, even move mountains.' He scowled and scratched his head. 'Now tell me this, Davie Campbell, what sane man would want to go around moving mountains?'

'I don't know,' Davie said frankly. It *did* seem an odd sort of pastime. He frowned and looked at the hermit. 'And where will I find the mustard seed, Mr Menzies?'

Old Tam sighed. He moved his head and shook his finger gently at the boy. 'It all comes from asking hard questions, Davie. We had it all taken care of just fine. Then you had to ask where you could find the mustard seed. That was the hard question that spoiled everything.'

'I'm sorry,' the boy said miserably.

'Never ask hard questions, Davie Campbell. Then if you don't get the right answer, you don't feel so bad.'

Davie nodded. It seemed to make sense. He was sorry he had asked Mr Menzies the hard question. Still, if he hadn't, how was he ever going to find the mustard seed that seemed to matter so much? It was all very confusing.

With Joseph romping at his heels, he made his way home, his mind an overturned beehive of quick, humming thoughts. Everyone thought the old hermit with the long white beard was crazy. But he knew differently. Tam Menzies was smart. Smart as a whip. Who else could have thought of saving Joseph with faith and mustard seeds? True, he had yet to find the mustard seed, but if he had faith he could.

He stopped. Faith? Somehow he had taken that part of it too much for granted.

He was just about to ask himself whether he had faith to believe that everything would be all right with Joseph. Then he remembered. Remembered what old Tam Menzies had said. Quickly he shook the thought from his mind.

Better not to ask any hard questions. Even of one's self. No telling what kind of answer he might get.

9

A Prayer for Joseph

Ian Campbell said grimly, 'So you failed even to give the beast away, eh, Davie?'

'Tam Menzies wanted him,' the boy said. He took his courage in his hands and looked straight at his father. 'And I want him myself.'

'Silence!' thundered Ian Campbell. With an effort he seemed to gain control of himself. Yet his voice was brittle with passion when he resumed.

'You are my son. You will do what you are told. When you are told. That beast is useless. I have already told you so. No one will take it. Even for nothing. No one except old Tam Menzies. And Christian that I am, I would turn no defenceless creature of God's over to a poor daft man.'

Davie looked at him, the misery in his eyes blurring his vision so that he could make out only the form of his father and a grim, harsh mouth. The words that he spoke were a thickness against his tongue, a strangeness in his ears.

'And if I'm not to keep Joseph and if there's no one to take him, what's to become of him?'

Ian Campbell hesitated. When he spoke, he spoke softly, almost gently. 'To set a poor wee beast loose in the hills would be cruel.' He looked at his son. 'We are not cruel, are we, Davie?'

The boy swallowed. 'No,' he said.

Ian Campbell nodded approval. 'I'm glad you understand that, lad. I would not want you to think I'm a hard man.'

Davie waited, silent.

'What's left for me to do, then, is best for the dog.' The big hands spread out in a gesture of helplessness. 'Best for the dog, aye, and everyone.'

'Best for—' Davie looked up quickly. The sudden sickness in his body made his legs tremble.

'Tomorrow,' said Ian Campbell quietly, 'I will take the dog up to the Angus River. And I will come home alone.'

'No!' Davie cried. 'You won't! You won't!'

'I won't?' Ian Campbell's face darkened.

'I'll take him myself.' He hadn't meant to say it, but now that it was said, it was better said. 'I'll take him myself,' he said again, only quieter this time.

'I see.' The grimness was still there on his father's face. 'So that we understand each other, what will you do in the morning?'

Davie did not look at him.

'I'll take him up—up—' His whisper collapsed under its burden of grief and when he opened his mouth there were no words there.

'To the hills,' prodded Ian Campbell.

'To the hills,' Davie repeated.

The eyes, bleak as mist, remained fixed on the boy.

'And place him in the river.'

'And place him'—he swallowed—'in the river.'

'Good.' The matter settled, Ian Campbell picked up a book and eased himself into his chair by the fire. He read in silence, his lips moving slightly as his eyes travelled across the fine lines of print. He seemed to have forgotten his son. Yet when he finally rose to go to his room he hesitated by the door, then called to Davie over his shoulder.

'I am a just man, Davie, as you know. And sometimes what we *must* do is not easy at all.' He paused and sighed a little and it was as though all the great strength in him had been used up, for there was a quietness in his voice when he spoke. 'Good night to you, Davie lad.'

Davie did not answer. The hatred in his heart for his father was a searing flame. Hatred for the cold eyes and the colder words. Hatred for this justice which he preached. Hatred for his world of useful things. A world wide enough to include shoes and plates and chairs and too narrow to hold a little dog.

He stumbled over to where Joseph lay in his box. The puppy wound a pink tongue around his finger as he lifted him up. And when Davie crept into bed, he took the dog with him and held him close in his arms.

He tried not to cry, but there was a queer stinging behind his eyes and when the tears came it felt better. And anyway if he cried a little, who cared, for the room was dark and no one could see. Except God, he reminded himself. And God didn't seem to care. Or did He?

His mind went back to his talk with old Tam Menzies. He was sorry there seemed no way to find the mustard seed. But surely if he just prayed, God would understand. Maybe that was where the faith came in. Maybe the thing that had moved the mountains had been the faith and not the mustard seed. Yes, that was it.

He never knew where the words came from but they were there on his lips and he spoke them.

'Oh Lord, I'm not asking You to move any mountains at all, unless it's Yourself has a mind to. And I'm not praying for Davie Campbell either. It's just wee Joseph here I'm thinking about. For he's got nobody at all but the both of us—You, Lord, and me, and I'm no help at all, at all. And oh,

I know how busy You are what with one thing and another and the world the way it is. But I thought, Lord, that Joseph being such a wee dog maybe You could spare a wee miracle. For it's a miracle he'll be needing if he's going to live. Aye, and we'll be thanking You greatly for it, will Joseph and me.'

Sleep came late to Davie but it came finally, came in a great rolling tide of mist. And it gathered Davie up in its arms gently and lovingly, just as Davie had gathered Joseph up in his, and bore him off to a land of dreamless peace.

10

Journey for Two

There was a small canvas bag near Davie's bed when he awoke. He did not have to ask who had left it, or what it was for. He tried not to look at it as he forced down the steaming plate of porridge that his mother gave him. The oatmeal, usually so smooth, seemed coarse against his tongue. Even the cold milk seemed flat and without taste.

When his mother's back was turned, he stole out

of the kitchen with Joseph. He sensed that this morning his mother would have kissed him. And had she done so, there was no saying what he might do. Why, he might even break out into tears!

Her back was still turned as he started to draw the door closed. He looked at her with eyes swimming with love and hurt. And then just as he stood there with his hand on the knob Joseph let out a small whinny of impatience. Davie froze. He waited for his mother to swing around and discover him. But she did not turn. Made no sign that she had ever heard. But she *must* have heard! It was only as he silently drew the door closed that he understood. His mother had read his heart. Had guessed at the tears behind his eyes. At his need to be alone. It was no accident that her back had been turned. No accident that she had not heard Joseph's whimper. And the tears that she did not see were bright in his eyes as he closed the door and slipped away from the cottage.

When Davie had arisen to find his father gone, his last hope to save Joseph had vanished. For how was Joseph to be spared if his father did not give the word? Now all that lay ahead was the bitter trip up the hills to where the Angus River flowed.

Only that and a certain task that made his heart sick to think about.

It had rained during the night, but with the morning the skies had cleared. As they passed under the giant sycamore outside the house the breeze from the hills sent a gentle spray of moisture down on the boy and the dog. Joseph shook himself and sniffed his annoyance. Little drops of rain dripped down his nose like tears.

Davie walked slowly. The wetness from the ferns was a coolness between his toes, but he did not feel it. The air was fragrant with the scent of meadowsweet and clover. He drew no pleasure from it. At the head of the glen Ben Ulva had doffed its nightcap of sullen cloud and now wore a rose-pink bonnet. Davie didn't even look at it.

Once Joseph sighted a rabbit and went off in instant chase. The rabbit outdistanced him in a matter of seconds. To Joseph, though, the whole thing was a mighty triumph. He trotted back to Davie, his long ears swaying gently like the sporran on a Highlander's kilt. It was his first victory over the enemy. Unless there were rabbits waiting to be chased in heaven, it might well be his last.

As they approached the steep incline Davie felt

his feet suddenly drag in the heather. He knew, with a terrible sureness, what lay beyond it. A frothing tumbling rush of peat-stained water. The Angus River.

Davie had almost reached the top of the steep hill when he noticed it. The stillness. The queer silence that made the hum of a bee loud in his ears. He stopped, wondering. Something was wrong. Was different. A solitary curlew flew past, trailing its mournful cry behind it. But that was all. Something was missing. Something familiar was gone. Something that belonged here. Then all at once in the sudden silence that closed in after the curlew's cry he knew what it was. He could not hear the Angus!

With a few quick bounds he crested the hill. He stopped short. The breath froze in his lungs at the sight that awaited him.

As far as his eyes could see the river was gone!

The Miracle

He stood for almost ten seconds where he was, his mind refusing to accept what his eyes beheld. It was impossible! The Angus had always been there. Had been there since time began. It was a part of the world itself. Like the sun and the moon and the stars. Its cheery gossip greeted every dawn. Its soft lullaby put every day to bed.

Slowly, as the shock grew less, Davie noticed other things. Although the river was gone, a deep brown channel remained, a channel of still pools and smooth flat rocks. Of long green reeds bending in chocolate-coloured mud. Of hundreds of round, white pebbles that gleamed in the sun.

'It's not to be believed at all,' he whispered in awe. Like one in a trance he walked across the bed of the river. The soft mud was a gentle coolness against his bare feet. It must have been like this, he thought, when Moses walked across the Red Sea with the Children of Israel. Only then the waters had been rolled back. Here they had been dried up.

Yet of one thing he was certain. God had heard

his prayer after all. And he had answered it. True, it *was* a little strange that he had gone to so much trouble to save one little dog's life. But who can tell about prayers anyway?

He watched as Joseph dashed at full speed through the small puddles in the river bed. His skinny little legs seemed to falter as the water broke against him. The next second he would burst through and strut proudly back to Davie, his tail like a battle standard, his small whiskers coated with glistening drops of moisture.

Davie's heart was light. He had put Joseph into the river just as he had been ordered. He had not disobeyed his father. And Joseph was alive—alive—alive!

He sang as he went home, and he noticed how the world had changed. How dreary it had seemed as he had made his way to the Angus. It couldn't just be the sun, for the sun had been shining before. Only now, somehow, it shone *differently*. With a new warmth and friendliness. It couldn't be the soft wind that smelled so sweet in his lungs. The wind had been there before. Only like the sun it was *different* now. The whole world was different now, full of rich gay colours and happy, happy

tunes. And as Joseph sported gaily at his heels the
song that he had sung that first day came to his lips.

> *Will ye no come back again,*
> *Will ye no, Prince Charlie?*
> *Better loved ye canna be,*
> *Will ye no come back again?*

And if Bonnie Prince Charlie had 'no come back
again,' at least Joseph had. Back to the world of
warm suns and soft hill winds. Back to the world
of rabbits to be chased and bones to be buried and
ears to be scratched.

Suddenly Davie stopped his whistling. There
was something else Joseph was coming back to.
Something dark and chilling and fearful.

The world of Ian Campbell.

12

The Grand Blood

Ian Campbell stopped when he saw Davie and
Joseph. With a big hand he swung the gate closed.
With the other he set the wooden milk bucket down
hard on the cobbled walk. His brow was black with
anger as the boy and the dog slowly approached.

'You have disobeyed me, Davie Campbell,' he said between tight lips. 'Aye, but what is worse, you have broken the word you gave me.'

Nell Campbell, alerted by the savage clatter of the milk bucket and the harsh voice of her husband, ran swiftly from the house. She bent down and threw her arms protectively around her son.

'You will not strike the lad, Ian,' she said quietly. 'I'll take care of this.'

The big farmer's eyes flashed. 'You will take care of a son who defies his father? A son who breaks his word?' His heavy breathing made his great chest rise and fall, rise and fall. 'I am a patient man, Nell Campbell. But I will not be mocked by my own son.'

'I did what you said,' Davie answered. 'Did I not give you my word?'

'Then what brings the dog back?'

Davie looked at his father, then hesitated. All of a sudden he realized something. How strange his story would sound to the ears of another. It takes faith to pray. It takes a stronger faith to believe that a prayer has been answered. His eyes wavered, then fell. He wet his dry lips with his tongue. He stared fixedly at the smooth cobbles. He did not speak.

'Answer me, boy!' thundered Ian Campbell.

Davie gulped and lifted his head. 'The Angus was not there at all,' he said in a small voice.

'What?'

Even his mother was looking at him queerly. He took a deep breath and went on. 'It's all dried up. There's no more Angus. Joseph—he ran all over where it had been.'

The tight, white lips separated just wide enough to let the words squeeze through. 'And on top of everything else, a liar besides!' His hand shot out and seized Davie roughly by the arm. 'How dare you come to me with such lies! How dare you!'

A stab of pain shot up Davie's arm where the fingers bit cruelly into his flesh.

'It's no lie I tell!' he cried. 'It's the truth! The truth. The Angus is dried up! Would I tell you if it was not so?'

'Aye, it's the truth Davie speaks. I just heard it now. The workmen on the Government project dammed it up. There's a new lake over by Ben Ulva.'

Ian Campbell wheeled round to face the speaker. Murdoch stood quietly and looked at his father. No one spoke for fully a minute.

'A new lake?' Ian Campbell finally said. He looked dazed. Slowly the pain slid from his eyes and down his face. Slowly his fingers gave up their fierce grip on Davie's arm. 'Then the lad did not lie at all?' he asked in a low voice.

'Is he not your son?' Nell Campbell said quietly.

'Aye,' he said slowly, 'he is that.' He seemed lost in thought. 'It will be strange with the Angus gone,' he mused after a pause. He spoke as though to himself. 'Many a grand day's fishing I had there when I was a lad.'

A quick dread chilled Davie's heart. 'I hope you're not minding that the Angus is gone!' he cried anxiously. 'I only asked for a wee miracle. Honest.'

His father was looking at him oddly. So was his mother. So was Murdoch.

'Miracle?' Ian Campbell said. 'You asked for a miracle?'

'Aye. I did. Last night.' He hastened on lest his father would misunderstand. 'But only a wee one. I never dreamed that God would be going to all this bother of drying up rivers.'

'But why, Davie?' It was almost a cry of anguish. 'Why did you want a miracle?'

'It was not for me,' Davie answered hurriedly. 'It was for Joseph.'

'Joseph?' Ian Campbell's face was grey.

Davie nodded. 'Aye, it seemed the only way to save Joseph.' Again he looked quickly at his father. 'But honest, I asked only for a wee miracle.'

For the longest moment Ian Campbell said nothing. And as he stood as though graven in stone, Davie noticed for the first time the depths of the lines around the mouth, the long streaks of silver in the dark hair. His father's voice when he spoke was soft with a softness Davie had never known.

He smiled a little sadly. 'Aye, Davie. God answers prayers in many ways. After all, does it not say in the Good Book itself that the Lord moves in a mysterious way His wonders to perform?'

Murdoch, who had stood watching the little drama, let a smile flit across his dark face. He ruffled his young brother's red hair. 'Now, Davie,' he said lightly, 'I can understand you having the river dried up and all, but why did you have to start moving mountains around? They must have blasted away half of Ben Ulva when they made that new lake up there.'

Davie stared. Wasn't that the very thing old Tam

Menzies said you could do when you had faith? Davie's mind reeled. How was he to have known what mighty forces he would set free last night when he had prayed for Joseph?

Murdoch laughed, then turned to his father.

'They say that the new Government power will be a fine thing for everybody. The electricity will help dry the hay and there will be more fodder for the cattle.' He turned and smiled with his eyes at his young brother. 'And maybe with better times and all we'll be needing some kind of dog around the place.' He scratched his head and looked wryly at Joseph. '*Any* kind of dog.'

Davie's heart skipped a beat. Anxiously he looked at his father. There was no expression on the gaunt face. The dark eyes were fixed on where Joseph lay on the cobbled walk, his chin resting trustingly on the farmer's rough boot.

Slowly Ian Campbell's body relaxed. Slowly he bent down. Slowly he drew a big clumsy finger down Joseph's back. 'Aye,' he said with a soft sigh of resignation, 'maybe it's right you are, Murdoch. Maybe it's right you are.'

The joy in Davie's heart was a winged, soaring thing. Joseph was his! His to keep and to love for ever and ever!

He threw himself down beside his father and never felt the stones that bruised his bare knees. He watched his father. His own wonderful, kind, understanding father. Somehow the sight of him patting the little dog filled him with a strange and marvellous warmth. And to think that it had only been a few days ago that he had thought he hated this man! Hadn't he been the foolish one! But it was different today. It would *always* be different. Perhaps that was part of the miracle too.

'And it's the great help he'll be to us,' he exulted, 'just wait and see. For it's a grand dog he is with the grand blood in him.' He looked at his father. 'Am I not right?'

Ian Campbell did not smile often. But he smiled now. A smile at once proud and humble. He put out his arm and he pulled his son close to him.

'Aye, the grand blood indeed,' he said.

Rory the Roebuck

DAVID STEPHEN

Illustrated by Don Higgins

I

Rory was born with his eyes open, unlike so many baby animals who are blind for some time after birth, so he was able to see the world round about him from the beginning. And he had plenty of time to look at it, for he had nothing else to do.

He was a handsome little fellow, and a delight to his mother's eyes. As in most roe deer families, Rory had a sister. She was a lovely, fairy-like creature, even smaller than Rory.

Rory was a buck fawn—which means he was the boy of the family—and his sister was a doe. They were very much alike to look at, and no mere human could have said which was which; but, of course, their mother always knew them right away.

Both had silky coats of foxy-red, and their flanks were covered with white spots like snowflakes. Their noses were black, moist and cool; their lower lips were white, and they had white marks on their upper lips. They had no tails. Their hooves were tiny, polished, and very sharp.

At the time this story opens Rory was only a few

hours old, and had not yet seen his sister. She was lying, curled up, in long dry grass about twenty yards from him. Rory's bed was a warm hollow, hidden by heather and birches. Both fawns were lying very still, and making no sound. Indeed, you might have thought they were not living things at all.

This business of lying still was most important for them. They were tiny creatures, no bigger than hares, not yet able to run with their mother, so they were safer lying still. All over the country thousands of baby deer were doing exactly the same thing.

Lying still, Rory and his sister were unlikely to be seen by fox or wildcat, or even by the eagle himself, for birds and beasts are not very good at spotting anything which is not moving. Of course, the four-footed hunters could smell. But Nature has given baby deer an advantage here, for while they are lying still they give off no body scent to betray them to their enemies.

Neither of the two fawns knew this; but they did know that they must lie still and quiet while their mother was away. That was the first law of survival.

Rory was eager to be up and doing things. The world looked such a wonderful place. But he did

not move. He kept his ears flat, not daring to twitch them, and he blinked his gentle eyes as seldom as possible. However, he was free to look and listen; so without realising it, he was learning much about the world he was living in.

The puffs of wind brought to his nose many exciting smells: the fresh smell of the earth, the balsamy fragrance of pines and spruces, the scent of heather. They were a bit confusing, for he didn't know which smell came from what, and it would be a little time before he was able to find out for himself.

The sounds were even more puzzling, especially the songs of the birds: cuckoos and thrushes, ravens and crows, grouse, curlews and peewits. He didn't even know yet what a bird looked like.

Suddenly a small lizard scurried past him, startling him for a moment. He breathed more quickly, so that his flanks heaved, but he did not move. The lizard whisked hither and thither, active in the warm sunshine. And, presently, it scurried off.

When, a little later, Rory heard a mouse rustling in the grass, he moved one ear to listen to it; but only for a moment. He didn't know what a mouse looked like, yet he was not afraid. In some strange way, which we do not understand, he knew the mouse was not dangerous.

The next sound he heard was his mother's footsteps. She was returning from her grazing to nurse her fawns. She was a small, slim deer, without any spots on her foxy coat. She had slender legs, a slender neck, jet muzzle and long ears which she kept wagging about, seeking sound of danger.

Rory and his sister scrambled to their feet, and saw each other for the first time. After they had suckled, Rory began to lick the milk smears from his sister's face, and in that way they became acquainted. Then they started to prance and caper round the doe, falling every now and again because they were still not very sure of their legs.

Their mother began to graze on the sweet grass while her fawns played round her. Every little while she tossed her head, to sniff the air and wag her ears, ever on the alert for any menace to her fawns. For perhaps ten minutes the roe family stayed among the birches, then the mother decided it was time for the fawns to lie down again.

She went to Rory's sister first, who lay down at once when she felt her mother's muzzle pressing

her rump. That was the doe's signal and the little fawn understood.

But Rory, being a buck, was made of different stuff. He knew perfectly well what he was supposed to do, but he just did not want to do it. He felt able to do anything an adult deer could do, so when the doe pressed him gently with her muzzle he tried to sneak away. However, his mother was relentless. She continued to press him, and once she tapped him with a dainty forehoof. Gradually, she pushed him down.

Rory didn't like this in the least, and he tried to struggle up again. But now his mother became firm with him. She butted him rather roughly, which surprised him, so he curled up and lay still.

For the next four hours the fawns did not move from their hiding places. The sun crossed the sky, bright and warm, and birds sang in the wood. The doe was out of sight, among the birches, resting and chewing cud just as cattle do. She could not see her fawns, but she knew where they were and was within earshot of them.

Roe deer are very cunning animals. When it was time for the doe to nurse her fawns again she came towards them with the wind blowing on her face.

In this way she was able to smell if there was any danger ahead. When she was quite satisfied that all was safe she walked slowly towards her family, calling to them:

'Whee-yoo! Whee-yoo! Whee-yoo!' she called, with her head low and her ears twitching.

'Eep-eep, nee-ee-eep!' the fawns answered her, and jumped to their feet.

They ran to her and in a moment were sucking greedily. They were now very much stronger on their legs, but not quite ready yet to run with their mother. So, after they had played for a short time, and tired themselves, they were put down again. And this time they lay down without complaint.

And now it was that Rory and his sister learned that there were other dwellers in the wood quite different from their gentle mother.

First, there was the big black crow, who flew into a low birch near the spot where the doe fawn was lying. He had a fir cone in his beak, and he began to play with it on a branch, holding it down with a foot while he pecked at it. He was bright-eyed and clever, and when Rory's sister wagged her ears to drive away a fly, he noticed the movement and soon picked her out.

Like most of his kind, he was a great bird for tomfoolery, and could be savage when he liked. Being in a playful mood, he flew down beside the fawn to peck at her and torment her. She, of course, knew nothing about crows, and when the big black bird tugged at one of her ears with his ebony beak she was afraid.

Still, she did her best to remain still, acting as though she were just part of the landscape and not a living thing at all. But the bright-eyed crow was not fooled for a moment.

He tweaked her other ear, and the fawn struggled. The struggling made the crow angry and he tried to peck her eye. This time she turned away her head and jumped to her feet. She stood there trembling until the crow pecked at her leg, then stumbled away from him, crying in distress.

A roe fawn has a cry like a small child, and the cry can be heard a long way off. Rory's mother, in her thicket, heard the fawn's cry. She knew at once that it was a cry of distress and she came bounding to the spot stamping in anger.

The crow knew better than to stay on the ground when he saw the doe coming. Instead, he flew into the birch tree and contented himself with mocking her from there. She reared up against the tree, dabbing at him with a forehoof, but she could not reach him. The bird bit off birch leaves and showered them down on her. Then he flew away cawing.

The doe went to her fawn and licked her with her warm tongue. The fawn whimpered at first, but she soon felt better, and nudged at her mother's flank. The doe then crossed to where Rory was lying and tapped him gently with a forehoof. She was bidding him rise and follow. Rory rose at once, glad to be on his feet, and the deer led both fawns from that part of the wood.

About two hundred yards from their old lairs they were put down again, this time in deep heather. They knew better than to protest, so they curled up without fuss, and again the doe left them to return to the thicket on the edge of the pines.

2

Now, it happened that there was a farm about half a mile away: a farm called Mossrigg. The farmer there was a big jovial man who was the friend of all the roe deer on his ground and would not let anyone harm them. He had a small terrier who also felt friendly towards deer, because she had once lived with a tame fawn which her master had reared on a bottle.

The dog was very fond of hunting rabbits, and she was forever on the prowl after rats, so it was not surprising that she should come trotting into the wood on one of her forays. And, as it turned out, she ran almost on top of Rory before she realised he was there.

The smell of the dog, and her fierce appearance, frightened Rory very much. He had no way of knowing that she was a friendly little dog, so he jumped to his feet in terror and began crying for his mother as his sister had done not long before. And again the doe came bounding from the wood.

She acted in good faith when she treated the dog as an enemy. She didn't know the terrier. All she knew was that she disliked dogs and had been chased by them many times in her life. Here she saw a new menace to her fawns. So she attacked with a great anger in her gentle heart.

The dog, of course, had no reason to fear deer. She had lived with a fawn for more than a year and was happy at finding what she thought was a new playmate. She could not understand that the fawn's mother might think otherwise.

As a result, she waited until the doe was almost on top of her before she realised that this was not the kind of deer she had been used to. The pounding hooves made that plain. So she turned and fled.

Rory was not hurt; but from that moment he learned that dogs had to be treated as enemies. His mother, by her behaviour, had made that clear. How could she, or Rory, possibly understand that they had just met the one dog in all the woods who would never have injured any deer?

Rory's mother now decided that this side of the wood was too dangerous for her fawns, so she struck them up and led them away to the thick scrub at the end. The distance was nearly half a mile and the fawns tired quickly. They were glad to lie down and rest when they arrived.

Rory and his sister slept twenty yards apart, and you may wonder why their mother chose to separate them like this. The explanation is simple. If a powerful enemy appeared on the scene, and they were side by side, both might fall a prey. Lying apart, there was every likelihood that one of them would be missed. The brown hare does the same with her leverets, giving each a separate form in the fields.

When Rory and his sister were six days old, their mother allowed them to run with her at night and she slept with them during the day.

That first day they kicked their heels, and pranced round their mother, delighted with their new freedom. Their lives were now really beginning. That night they saw fox and badger for the first time. The badger went about his business, but the fox skulked around until the doe drove him off with grunts and stabbing hooves.

At sunrise the fawns lay down to rest, for they had been on foot most of the night. The doe wandered into the wood a little distance to drink. After half an hour Rory began to fret at her absence, but he lay quite still. When he heard voices and loud bangs in the wood he was a little frightened, and longed for his mother. But he did not move.

Much later—long after the sun had passed its peak—he began to cry for his mother. He rose and, still crying, looked for her in the wood. But he could not find her. That evening, and throughout the windy night, he called for her, and his sister joined him with her plaintive cry. But their mother did not come. She would never come again.

The fawns, of course, didn't know what had happened to her. They knew only the loss of her. They did not know that men existed, or what guns were, so how could they understand that their mother had been taken from them?

By daylight Rory's sister had wandered away, running and calling until she was exhausted, before lying down in a thicket where she fell into a heavy sleep. Her sleep became the deep, kindly sleep which Nature brings to the helpless, so that they know no more distress.

Rory did not wander. He lingered among the birches, calling at intervals, and lying down frequently to rest. In ordinary circumstances he would have died, either by sleeping away, like his sister, or falling, mercifully, a prey to fox, or wildcat, or eagle. But to Rory, as sometimes happens in such cases, help came in the shape of the roe deer's greatest enemy—man!

His cries were heard that morning by John Long, the keeper, as he was going his rounds. Knowing his woods, and having trained ears, the keeper was able to plot the spot at once, and in a few minutes he was standing beside the motherless fawn.

By then, Rory's tongue was cold, which is a sure sign that a roe fawn is near collapse, and John Long realised at once that the little beast at his feet was far gone.

At first he was tempted to do the humane thing: to tap the little fawn on the head and have done with the whole tragic business. Then he thought what a wonderful pet the fawn would make for his girl Susan, if only he could be kept alive!

Rory, despite the warmth of the day, was cold, for young animals deprived of milk lose heat quickly. John Long knew that warmth was as essential as nourishment, so he gathered the fawn comfortably in his green tweed jacket and set off through the wood in the direction of his cottage. His bundle hindered him not at all, for he was a big man with the strength of a horse, and Rory was a tiny fawn, no heavier than a cat.

During the journey Rory did not make the slightest movement; he was in a kind of coma, only dimly aware of what was happening to him. John Long did not like the way his tongue was showing at the side of his mouth.

When the keeper reached home he deposited his

bundle gently on the kitchen table.

'Here's a roe fawn,' he said to his wife. He un-wrapped Rory, laid his jacket aside, and shook his head. 'But it'll need magic, I'm thinking.'

Mrs Long, however, was a practical woman, and she soon had Rory bedded in a big dog basket, with two hot-water bottles, and covered with a light blanket. Rory breathed deeply and steadily in the engulfing warmth, and presently he opened his eyes.

The keeper forced a few drops of his best whisky between Rory's lips, and watched the ears begin-ning to prick and the tired eyelids flutter. He gave the fawn a few more drops, and soon Rory was sighing happily and wrinkling his nose.

But, try as they might, neither the keeper nor his wife could persuade the fawn to take milk from bottle or teaspoon. He cried and struggled, till he was panting with exhaustion. The keeper was greatly worried. Reviving the fawn with whisky would not do much good if he refused to take milk.

It was Susan, arriving breathless from school, who solved the problem.

3

Susan was delighted when she saw the fawn, then almost in tears when she realised how dangerously weak he was. Though her parents warned her not to touch the animal, she had Rory and hot-water bottles in her lap the moment their backs were turned. And when they looked round they saw the fawn vigorously sucking their daughter's thumb.

And that was really how Susan solved the problem. She dipped her thumb in milk, and Rory sucked. She dipped again, and Rory sucked her wet thumb greedily. Susan kept wetting her thumb, and Rory kept sucking. He had to do much sucking for little milk, but the little milk put strength into him.

So his life was saved. It was not really difficult after that to get him to take milk from a teaspoon. Susan managed it by allowing him to suck spoon and thumb together a few times. Rory soon discovered where the milk was and presently pushed her thumb out of the way altogether.

In three days he was skipping about the kitchen.

After a week he was prancing upstairs to Susan's bedroom. In six weeks he was bouncing on to the ferret hutches and the garden shed. And now, as far as he would ever know, Susan was his mother.

He followed her everywhere. He went for walks with her, slept on a sheepskin rug beside her bed, and ate with her at table, with his tiny forehooves in her lap. To Susan's father he looked for cigarettes, which he ate with relish; to her mother he looked for pancakes, spicy biscuits and other delectable things. Pancakes, especially, he ate with unending delight, and he would tap Mrs Long's apron with a forehoof to indicate he wanted more.

The keeper's four big dogs—Tweed, Tam, Tarf and Tearlach—loved him and gave him their protection, sharing in his capers and putting up with his prodding without growl or grimace. The dogs became utterly devoted to him, and would chase after him in the fields until their tongues were hanging out.

One day, when a roving lurcher dog gave chase to Rory in the paddock, Tarf rushed between them, shielding the fawn against her flank whilst big Tweed, the fearless, drove the intruder back to the woods.

Rory and Susan played together through the long summer holidays, and when the sun was bright you could not have separated their shadows. Then the time came for Susan to return to school, and Rory was left to amuse himself by day. He gambolled with the dogs, especially Tweed his protector, and chased the cats, but he missed Susan.

For the first few days after her return to school he fretted a good deal until he realised that, each evening, at a certain time, she would return. In those first days he eased his fretting on anything within reach. He butted the rose bushes, the apple trees, the rooster and the gander. He prodded at the ferrets in their hutches. And, when he wanted to go into the house, he butted the door with his head, angrily.

In September, his baby spots disappeared, and when the leaves were falling he grew a new coat of warm grey, with twin white patches on his gullet. This was his first winter dress.

Susan's father was certain Rory would now go back to the woods, thinking that surely he must feel the urge to join his own kind. But winter came and Rory was still at the cottage, skipping about as usual, wandering to the woods in the evening but always returning at daybreak each morning. The keeper then gave him until spring; but spring came to prove him wrong, for Rory was still there.

When the chestnut buds were sticky with varnish, Rory had short, sharp antler spikes, and he became very haughty, lording over everything except his good friends the dogs. And still he stayed. When Susan's holidays came round again he was still there to romp with her in the fields and woods as before.

But, after about two weeks, he became restless. He began to disappear for a day at a time. And there were mornings when Susan listened in vain for his knock at the door. Sometimes he stayed away for a whole day and a night, wandering in the woods on his own secret affairs.

'One of these days he won't come back at all,' said the keeper.

'You had better warn Susan, then, and explain that the day is bound to come when he will want to leave for ever,' said Mrs Long.

When it finally did happen, Susan's father told her: 'He's gone back to his own kind. It had to happen some day, and you can't really blame him. It's the call of the woods.'

But Susan, deeply hurt, could not believe that Rory would desert her completely. So she looked for him—in the near woods and out to the edge of the moor—right through the golden September days. But she could not find him. Then October came, with no Rory. And, presently, she stopped looking.

Rory did not travel far on his first day out—no further than the big wood. He followed a well-marked deer path out to the heather, and lay up in a warm fern brake for the day. He was now in strange country.

Before nightfall he rose from his bed and crossed the heather, then followed a sheep path down a rocky slope to the river.

After he had eaten his fill of sweet grass, and nibbled at golden aspen leaves, he lay down to chew cud in a sheltered hollow, where he was hidden from everything except the sun. The sun came up, glaring and hot as it can in October, and soon the flies came out to torment him. To escape them he trotted uphill to a heathery knoll, where the fresh breeze kept them away.

He liked the river, and the thickly wooded valley,

so he stayed there for several days, until he had an unfortunate experience which made him move on.

One morning he saw a man walking along the river bank, with a gun under his arm and a brown-and-white dog at heel. Rory did not run away because he looked upon men and dogs as his friends. But when the man fired a shot at him he bounded headlong towards the forest, with a new fear in his heart and a stinging pain in his rump.

Luckily for Rory, he was almost out of range before the gun was fired. He was hit by only two pellets which made small punctures in his hide. They stung him but did no serious injury, and after a day or two he forgot all about them. Strangers and dogs he would never forget.

A day's journey brought him to another valley, and the greatest forest he had yet seen. It stretched right along the mountainside, up to the high ridges, which were the haunt of the wildcat and the eagle. And it was here he met the first roe deer he had seen since the day the keeper found him.

The deer was a young buck, only five months old, and not long out of his baby coat. He was nibbling at aspen leaves when Rory approached. Rory was glad to meet one of his own kind, so his greeting was friendly, and when they had touched noses they ran into the forest together, shaking heads and kicking heels.

But the young buck had a mother—a slim doe, red as a fox, who stamped her foot angrily when she saw the strange deer with her fawn. The white patch on her rump opened out like a flower, betraying her alarm, then she realised Rory was young and friendly and came to meet him. After they had touched noses, they began to graze.

Rory was happy with his new friends, and the doe treated him as she would have done her own yearling. For two days they lived quietly as a family, feeding from nightfall until dawn, and lying up most of the day. Then the old buck appeared.

He was five years old, haughty and with white-tipped antlers more than nine inches long. At the sight of Rory he was fired with jealousy. For a moment he stood tossing his head, and tapping with a forehoof, then, with a loud grunt, he rushed to the attack.

In some way Rory understood that the old buck was dangerous, so he didn't wait to be stabbed by the sharp, nine-inch horns. He leaped aside, and bounded into the forest, kicking up twigs and fir cones, turning and twisting whenever the old buck pressed him too close. He was panting, with tongue showing, before his pursuer tired of the chase and returned to his doe and fawn.

That escapade taught Rory to respect older bucks, but it did not frighten him off. He had grown to like the company of the doe and her fawn. So he waited for dusk, then circled back warily to find them, moving stealthily from tree to tree so that he would not be seen.

He found them on the hill, nibbling at blaeberry leaves on a knoll. The fawn ran to him, calling 'Eep-eep!' At the sound, the buck turned from his browsing, threw up his head, stamped with a foot, and wagged his ears. He was no longer really angry, and soon returned to his blaeberries, which he found more interesting than young whipper-snappers like Rory.

Rory was glad to be accepted again. The doe sniffed him over, and nuzzled his neck. But the buck remained aloof, and Rory did not go too near him in case he lost his temper again. The fawn, on the other hand, took great liberties with the old buck, butting him on the flank, prancing round him, and tapping him with a hoof. But, of course, the buck was his father, and that made it different.

From ignoring Rory, the old buck grew to tolerating him close at hand, and, after a week, accepted him as a member of the clan. And no human could have told that Rory was the stranger in the family.

4

Each night could be heard the roaring of the great red stags which lived on the hill, and sometimes in the moonlight Rory saw tall, dark shapes, with high, branching antlers, challenging each other to combat. The big stags ripped the heather with their antlers, and rolled in peaty waterholes, until they were wet and plastered with mud. This was the rutting, or mating, season of the red deer, and Rory was careful to avoid the big stags while they were in such a mood.

During his nightly forays in search of food he met other animals who were his neighbours. There was the badger, squat and grey, with bristly hair and white-striped face, who came through the forest each night to go foraging on the hill. He was a powerful animal who had no quarrel with anyone. Rory often met him at night, when the badger would turn his head to look at him, then grunt and move on, bear-like but with the movements of a weasel.

There was the big wildcat from the high cairns —wide in the skull, flat-eared and green-eyed, with short, blunt tail ringed with black. She always hissed and spluttered at sight of Rory, and he kept close watch on her, knowing her to be dangerous. But she had much respect for his hooves, and did no more than crackle at him spitefully.

There were the hares of the mountains, blue-coated and white-footed, who went quietly about their affairs, and often grazed alongside the deer. And there were the stoats, smaller kin of the badger, always ready to spit and chatter at any living thing. For some reason Rory did not like the stoats, and any time he saw one he gave chase, striking at it with his forehooves.

Then there was the big dog fox who came nightly from the hill to hunt the forest edge. He was a big beast, almost half as big again as any lowland fox, long-jawed and lean, with red legs and a white-tipped brush. Rory was always on guard against him, having apparently some kind of inherited wisdom concerning foxes.

By day, there was the eagle, soaring high above the mountains, but Rory saw little of her, and that was only when the bird was on the ground. The ravens he came to know better, because they were forever flying to and fro, seeking carrion, pitching here and there, and sometimes feeding close to the deer. When a raven croaked, Rory paid attention, because they were wise birds, ever ready to give the alarm at the first hint of danger.

In the forest Rory made the acquaintance of the giant capercaillies: the great wood grouse, big as turkeys, who fed on the green shoots of pine trees, and roosted in the highest branches. There, too, he met the blackcocks, who were also forest dwellers, although they spent much of their time on the open hill.

Such were his neighbours, and he had little trouble with most of them. But one day, when he was out on the hill feeding alongside the old buck, the eagle taught him that danger could come from the air.

Down from the blue she came, in a dizzy dive, a feathered thunderbolt hurtling earthwards, with

the wind hissing in her wings. Rory saw her shadow, and heard the wind in her wings, before he looked up to discover the cause. And there she was, almost on top of him! Swoosh! She was down. Rory twisted away, his hair no more than scratched by the clutching foot. Then, swoosh! the eagle was up again, keeling over for a second attack.

In panic, Rory bounded to the old buck's side, and pressed against his flank. The eagle came down a second time, and the two bucks leaped aside, eluding her. Once again the eagle threw herself up, then round, and down, swooping at Rory with talons set to grapple.

And now the old buck showed his mettle. As the eagle came in he reared on his hindfeet to meet her. His forehoof struck her on a wing, piercing the feathers and splitting the webs. Jerked off balance the eagle lurched away, fighting for control. The shock sent the old buck over on his back, but he was on his feet again in time to see the eagle circling wide, in controlled flight, before she began soaring back to her pitch.

During November Rory spent much time in the open, on his own, joining the buck, with his doe and fawn, at dusk when they came from the forest to graze. One night the old buck appeared without antlers, and Rory was so perplexed he went over to smell the spot where they had been. In their place the buck had two raw sores. He had cast his old antlers, and would soon begin growing new ones.

Rory, on the other hand, being younger, would keep his short antler spikes until the end of the year, for that is the way of it with roe deer. But if he had any ideas about being the master buck of the family he was soon disillusioned. The old buck still had his forehooves, and they were deadly weapons. Once, losing his temper with Rory, he struck out with a foot. Rory moved aside just in time, for the stroke would have cut him deeply. His respect for the old buck was restored, and there were no further incidents of the kind.

In December the hill tops were white, and each night the whiteness spread downwards after new flurries of snow. The wind blew from the northeast, icily, and frost came with the sunset to harden the ground and whiten the heather. The deer fed in the forest when the frost was on the grass, and lay out by day, in sheltered hollows which caught the sun.

Rory, born and reared on the low ground, where the woods were warm and the winds less keen, began to tire of this wild, open hill country, with its bleak valleys and searching cold. He kept more and more to the forest, where there was shelter and good grass. But he was fond of browsing on birch and aspen twigs, and when he wanted these he had to leave the forest and seek out the gorges where they grew.

In mid-December he left the hill, after an adventure in a gorge where he had been browsing on birch twigs. There was only one way in and out of the gorge; at one end the rocks formed a steep crag up which a wildcat could not have climbed. Rory was feeding under the crag when the musk-taint of fox came to his nose on the wind.

The smell did not alarm him at first. He had sniffed fox-taint many times and was not afraid of it. When the smell came stronger and stronger he turned to view the fox, and there in front of him, barring the exit, were two mountain foxes, long-legged and powerful, with eyes slitted and tongues a-loll.

They did not come forward, or go back when he stamped. They just stood there, grinning foxy grins. Perhaps they hoped to stampede him. Perhaps, if he stampeded, he would jump about wildly, and injure himself, allowing them to come in chopping. That is what they were planning. They liked venison, fresh or carrion. And they liked planning. But their plans came to nothing.

At first, Rory was tempted to panic, and do just what they wanted him to do. Then the fire kindled in him. He stamped with a forehoof, and that made the foxes just a little uneasy. He grunted, and tossed his head, and that made them hesitate. But before they could make up their minds to withdraw Rory rushed at them.

They had barely time to leave their seats before his hooves were dabbing where they had been. Right out of the gorge Rory pursued them, stabbing at their rumps, then bounding ahead and trying to dirk them with his antler spikes. They were, of course, as nimble as he, but they had to use all their wits to keep clear. When they at last escaped in a jumble of rocks they were two badly frightened foxes.

That incident decided Rory, and without waiting for daylight, or seeking out the old buck and his family, he set off through the forest, heading for the moors, which his instinct told him were his home.

5

Below a thousand feet there was no snow, but the frost had the earth in its grip, and grass and heather were white. Before daybreak, loping through thickets of frosted rhododendrons, Rory reached the river where he had been shot at nearly ten weeks earlier. The riverside trees were stripped of their leaves, the tussocks matted and bleached by frost and icy winds, and the only bird sound was the scolding of jays in the spruces on the far bank.

Rory snipped twigs from the riverside alders, and chewed, twirling them between his lips. Then he muzzled into tussocks to uncover grass free from frost, and filled his paunch. The morning was sunless, with chill mists crawling through the trees. Rory splashed across the river and loped into the spruce gloom to rest and chew cud.

He chose a dense tree, with low, down-pointing fronds, and lay on the dry earth underneath, his breath vapouring as he chewed. His sides heaved comfortably. He was content.

At mid-morning the mists lifted, but clouds hid the blue of the sky. Rory, from his lair, had a clear view of the river for some distance upstream and down; the wind was playing on his back, so he was able to smell where he was not looking. He kept watch along the river, remembering the man with the gun.

This time no man appeared, but presently the watchful deer spied a black-and-white collie trotting along the near bank, sniffing at holes and under tree roots. He was out rabbiting for sport which, of course, Rory could not know. Rory stopped chewing and, with ears pricked and opened forward, kept his eyes on the dog.

The collie trotted on, with his pink tongue hanging out, and his feathery tail wagging: a working sheepdog who also herded cattle, liked cats and chased only rabbits. But he was a new-comer to the district, and had never met a deer. And a deer is a sore temptation for any dog, however hard-working or well-trained.

Rory's line from the river was cold—which is to say his scent no longer lay where he had walked—so the dog crossed it without any sign of excitement. But the wind blowing on Rory's back was carrying his scent to the river, and presently the dog reached the point where he could smell the hidden deer.

Now he became excited. He whined, pointed his nose high, and sniffed. The smell was new and intriguing. He decided to find out where it came from and what caused it, so with his nose high and his tail feathering he padded straight for Rory's hiding-place.

Rory knew at once that he had been discovered, and he jumped to his feet. But he did not run. Although he was himself only the size of a doe, being under two feet high, he had reached the stage, which almost all roebucks reach sooner or later, when he was afraid of no single dog the size of a collie, so long as there was no man accompanying it. Instead of running away he walked from the spruces and stood in full view waiting for the dog.

The collie was so engrossed following his nose that he did not see the deer until he was within a few yards; then it was the movement of Rory, stamping and shaking his head, that he noticed. He stopped short, whining, and reaching out with his nose, trying to puzzle out what kind of animal Rory was. He knew he was no sheep or cattle beast. So what was he?

Training, and discipline, prevented him from rushing at any living creature without being told. But Rory's smell was terribly exciting to his nostrils. He quivered with the urge to chase, but was restrained by habit. And eventually he sneaked away, with a shame-faced air, as though he had been caught in the act of committing a crime.

In one way, Rory's experience with the collie was unfortunate; it gave him a dangerous contempt for dogs. A few days later, when he was out on the moor, his contempt almost cost him his life.

He was lying in the heather, in the lee of a peat hummock, when he heard the swish and crackle of feet behind him. Jumping at once to his feet, he saw a big lurcher, part collie, part greyhound, turning short after a hare which was expending its last breath trying to escape. Instead of fading quietly away, then running, Rory stood watching, stamping with a forehoof.

The lurcher caught his hare, and was on the way back to his master in the wood, when he winded the deer. In the next instant he placed Rory standing there. Dropping the hare the lurcher rushed at Rory: a tall, rangy dog, long-jawed, more than a match for any deer of the size.

In that life-or-death moment Rory realised his mistake. This was no good-natured sheepdog. This was a killer. With a tremendous bound Rory leaped straight at the onrushing lurcher. Right over the dog's head he sailed. And because the dog had to turn about to chase, he lost ground, and he was fifty yards behind before he got into his stride.

Rory bounded for the spruce wood, where the thick trees would hide him and slow down the dog, for no dog can keep pace with a deer in dense cover. He reached the wood, with an increased lead, but the lurcher kept on his track unerringly, hunting now by scent, and Rory knew then that he was running for his life.

He left the wood and splash-trotted across the river, raced down-stream and down the wind, and splashed back again into the spruce cover. When he had done this three times the lurcher was beaten. Good though his nose was he could not unravel Rory's trail. So he gave up at last, and returned to the moor to find his hare, while Rory, panting, stood neck-deep in the river under screening alders.

Rory left the river that night, feeding as he travelled, crossing pastures and frozen ploughland, resting in gorse brakes or birch thickets, but always heading in the direction of his old home. A flurry of snow from the east spotted him with white, but the wind died quickly, and the sky cleared, and he shook the spots from his hair. By midnight he was in the big wood, Ravenscraig, six miles from Glencryan where he was born.

He lingered in Ravenscraig during the day, because he was upset after his chase by the dog. For a while he browsed on birch twigs and willow tips, and when he had paunched full on these he lay down to rest.

But Ravenscraig could not hold him now. The cover in the wood was good, and there was plenty of grass, but he was so near his home ground that he had to be moving. He left Ravenscraig in daylight, crossing the heather at a slow walk, and stopping only to scratch an ear with a hindfoot or rake his flank with an antler tip.

Out on the heather he passed roe from his home range, obviously disturbed by something because they were looking back the way they had come. Rory could find no scent of danger on the crosswind, so he went on. He had not the fears of the wild deer who knew only the life of the woods, and Glencryan, his home wood, was near at hand.

Before he reached it snow was falling, in great swirling flakes, silently.

6

It was a few days before Christmas, and at John Long's cottage everybody was busy with preparations. The keeper had given his daughter Susan a small model of a roebuck for her tree, and she was so delighted with her present that she had to re-arrange the lights. She wanted the model to have two to itself. Her father smiled, knowing he had touched the right chord.

When she had nearly finished the decorations and the tree was ablaze with the many-coloured lights, Susan remembered the holly.

'Daddy! You've forgotten the holly!' Then, as an afterthought, born of impatience, she added, 'Never mind. I'll get it myself.'

'It's a tidy step,' her father warned. 'Leave it until tomorrow and I'll go myself.'

But Susan was determined and, clad in coat, scarf and gloves, she set out on her bicycle in the middle of the afternoon for Glencryan Wood. Three miles and a bit were nothing to Susan.

When she reached Glencryan the wind was blowing from the east, threatening snow. Warm after her journey, Susan put her gloves into the

basket on her handlebars, and wheeled her bicycle into the cover of a big spruce not far from the road. Then she set off along the woodside, skirting the boggy places, towards the big hollies with their abundant berries.

The first snow was drifting down like tit feathers when she spied the roe out on the moor—five of them, moving away at an easy lope. When they stopped to look back, Susan started out after them. Was it possible that one of them might be her beloved Rory? Of course, the roe moved on again; and, just as surely, their curiosity made them stop before they would run another two hundred yards. Susan, ready to turn when they moved away, could not resist following when they stopped.

Four times the roe deer stopped and moved on and Susan suddenly realised she was far out on the moor, and that the snow was now beginning to swirl down in great fluffy flakes. So she turned, and started to run for the shelter of the Glencryan spruces.

But the snow fell, thick and silent, blotting out the trees in a swirling chaos. Panic seized Susan. She could not see where she was going. She slipped, stumbled and fell when the heather snagged her feet. The snow drifted down steadily in a witch's dance that defeated all vision and sense of direction, and darkness was falling when Susan at last reached the first trees.

She didn't know what part of the wood it was, and she was helpless in the swirling snow. The spruces became draped in ermine wraps. Susan began to cry. Her feet were now cold, and she could feel the first chilling wetness on her spine.

Determined, she tried to find her way from the wood. But Glencryan—the Glencryan she thought she knew so well—was now a strange land, and she was bewildered by the unceasing snow-swirl. In her panic she fell over a half-buried tree, jarring her shoulder and cutting her forehead deeply. When she struggled to her feet, her crying was the crying of terror.

She was leaning against a tree, sobbing violently, when she felt a light touch on her arm. The light touch became a heavy one, and fear gripped Susan, of a kind she had never before known. She turned, screaming, and covered her face with her hands. Then, suddenly, she was babbling:

'Rory! Rory! Dear Rory! I knew you'd come!' And she hugged fiercely the slender neck, while

Rory's velvet muzzle sniffed her hair.

Walking, with her hand grasping the hair of Rory's neck, she was conscious of cold and confusion and pain. But her fear was gone. Rory plodded along slowly, stopping now and again to nibble at twigs, leading her through the woods and fields.

For Rory there was really no problem, for he remembered that he had been walking with Susan before. Which way did he go? To the cottage, of course! He had done it many times before. He would do it again. Of course Rory did not think all this out; he did not think at all. Indeed, he had no idea that Susan was lost. He was simply going back with her, now that he had found her in the wood.

They were far across country, plodding over the snow, when the search party, headed by Susan's father, reached Glencryan. So they were missed, and Susan saw no lights and heard no voices. She walked in a kind of trance, and Rory had her on the road, three hundred yards from home, without her being aware of it.

Suddenly he broke away from her, and vanished over the roadside dyke, with a farm collie barking at his heels. And, in a moment, Susan was crying again, feeling deserted and not knowing where she was.

But this time she was heard by two searchers who had just left the cottage: two men with lamps and what seemed to Susan the most wonderful voices in the world. 'My goodness, wean! Where have you been?' said one, as he gathered her in his arms.

Susan's mother, almost out of her wits with worry, burst into tears when the men took the sobbing girl home. But Mrs Long was no weakling. Right away she telephoned for the doctor, and soon she had Susan tucked up in bed, with hot-water bottles round her. But she was puzzled by the girl's unceasing calls for Rory.

When the doctor examined the patient, and listened to her confused whimpering, he turned to Mrs Long. 'She's delirious,' he said. 'She's had a frightening experience, and will need watching. I'll see her tomorrow.' And he gave Susan something to make her sleep.

Though she knew that Susan was injured, and in a highly nervous state, Mrs Long was not at all sure about the delirium. She had a funny feeling about Susan's story. Her husband agreed it was all quite possible, but why had the men not seen any sign of Rory or found any of his tracks in the snow? And why had Rory not come to the cottage?

By Christmas Eve Susan was much better but she still had to stay in bed. Her wounds were healing quickly, and she had almost forgotten about her bruised shoulder. Her bed was brought downstairs, so that she could be near her Christmas tree.

Outside the snow lay deep and frozen. In the dark blue sky the stars winked icily. Susan thought of the dark trees of Glencryan, and Rory. Presently, some of her school friends would be arriving to cheer her up.

'It was Rory who found me,' she kept saying to her mother. 'He was there. He brought me home.'

'We know, dear,' her mother said kindly. 'But just don't excite yourself. He heard you crying and came to you.'

To her husband she whispered: 'I wonder . . . and, anyway . . . I want to believe it.'

John Long spoke to Susan later, and he was most serious. 'Susan,' he said, 'when your friends come, I wouldn't tell them . . . about Rory, I mean . . . not yet anyway. There's my girl!'

Susan did not tell them. She had her tray in bed, while her father and mother sat at the table with her friends. The keeper made jokes, and told stories, but the atmosphere remained strained. Somehow, it just did not seem right to be merry with Susan lying in bed.

Suddenly, the terrier on the hearth pricked her ears and growled deep in her throat. Outside, the big dogs in the kennels started to bark. In the house everyone fell silent, and stopped eating, to listen. There was a commanding tap-tap-tap at the back door.

'It'll be the doctor,' John Long said, though he wondered why the doctor should come on Christmas Eve. 'I'll answer it.'

But it was not the doctor at the door, and no doctor in the world was ever more welcome than the visitor who entered.

'Rory!' cried Susan.

In came a prancing roebuck, grey-coated and damp with frost, shaking his head and plainly pleased to be there. He skidded round the table, taking half the carpet with him, and pulled up short at Susan's bed.

'Rory! Rory!' she cried in shrill delight. 'You've

come! Oh, Mummy . . . Daddy . . . you see . . . it *was* Rory. I told you so.' And she began all over again, trying to tell them everything at once.

Susan's mother hugged Rory, and cried over him. Then she laughed when he snatched a piece of cake from the hand of one of Susan's friends.

'Same old Rory!' She petted him, while her carpet was decorated with crumbs. 'Come on, everyone. Wish Rory a very Merry Christmas!'

They did so, patting and hugging him, but Rory was too intent on Susan's tray to heed them, and eventually he finished up on the bed beside her. Then, suddenly, he leaped to the floor again, rushed up to the keeper and began nosing at his pocket.

John Long laughed, pulled out his cigarette case, and offered one to Rory. Rory accepted it gently and ate it on the spot, much to the delight and amazement of the children.

'Merry Christmas, Rory,' the keeper said, and gave him another cigarette. 'I see you haven't given up the tobacco habit while you've been away.'

Mrs Long disappeared into the kitchen, and

presently she returned with a tray of beautiful newly-made pancakes.

'Merry Christmas, Rory,' she said. And she gave him the entire tray.